# Keep*t!*

Written by Carolina Ortega
Illustrated by Diane Paterson

 ScottForesman

*A Division of* HarperCollins*Publishers*

When we march down the street. . .

we snap our fingers,
snap, snap, snap.

We clap our hands,
clap, clap, clap.

We slap our hips,
slap, slap, slap.

We tap our toes,
tap, tap, tap.

When we march down the street,

we make music with a
snap-tap beat.